Thomas Patrick Faulkner

**The Career of George Robert Fitzgerald**

Better known as Fitzgerald the Fire-eater, in the West of Ireland

Thomas Patrick Faulkner

**The Career of George Robert Fitzgerald**
*Better known as Fitzgerald the Fire-eater, in the West of Ireland*

ISBN/EAN: 9783337060404

Printed in Europe, USA, Canada, Australia, Japan

Cover: Foto ©Raphael Reischuk / pixelio.de

More available books at **www.hansebooks.com**

# GEORGE ROBERT FITZGERALD,

BETTER KNOWN AS

## FITZGERALD THE FIRE-EATER,

IN THE

## WEST OF IRELAND.

BY

THOMAS PATRICK FAULKNER, B.A., LL.B.,

• *Barrister-at-Law,*

CONNAUGHT CIRCUIT, CASTLEBAR.

# PREFACE.

—◆—

IN presenting this work to his Readers, the Author hopes that they will not pronounce their verdict solely on whatever drawbacks that may appear in its pages, but that the dearth of literature on the subject and the difficulty of collecting tradition will also be in evidence.

However, he adds that no pains have been spared to test the Historical and Geographical references ; that old magazines, mouldy documents, and obliterated manuscripts have been assiduously and exhaustively investigated ; and that the Reader is always put on his guard when treading on the domain of Fable or Romance as opposed to Fact.

It is only fair to acknowledge the valuable assistance the Author received from an eminent scholar in Irish Antiquities, George Dames Burtchaell, Esq., M.A., LL.B., Barrister-at-Law and Treasurer of the Royal Society of Antiquarians, Ireland ; and also from an old and esteemed friend, John D. O'Hanlon, Esq., Barrister-at-Law and Treasurer of the King's Inns, Dublin, a gentleman whose marvellous memory contains a store of varied antiquarian erudition.

THE AUTHOR.

# CONTENTS.

---

## CHAPTER I.

## CHAPTER II.

## CHAPTER III.

## CHAPTER IV.

# THE CAREER OF

# GEORGE ROBERT FITZGERALD

IN THE

# WEST OF IRELAND.

————◆————

## CHAPTER I.

The Times—State of Society—Duelling—Birth of George Robert—
Village of Turlough—Turlough Castle—Turlough Round Tower—
His Parents—George Robert at Eton.

IT is a strange, yet a notorious fact that some of the most
interesting scenes enacted in Connaught during the last
century, and some of the most striking characters in those
scenes have escaped the pen of the Historian. The unre-
corded events that occurred during the latter half of
the eighteenth century in Mayo, Sligo, and Galway would
furnish ample matter for a bulky volume, and certainly an
entertaining one; no person, however, has, as yet, under-
taken the task, nor is it necessary to inform the Reader that
no attempt to meet this want is contemplated here. To
sketch in four brief chapters the career of George Robert
Fitzgerald in Mayo: his birth, duels, trial and execution is
all the author designs.

I draw my information from the following sources princi-
pally :—Sir Jonah Barrington's " Personal Recollections ; "
Hamilton Rowan's " Autobiography ;" Mathew Arch-
deacon's " Legends of Connaught." I have had the good
fortune of hearing much concerning the freaks of our hero
in Castlebar, from the lips of very old persons who received
their information from contemporaries of George Robert.

## The Times.

To be able to form a just estimate of his character ; to
be fair in dealing out censure as well as eulogy, it will be
necessary to have a picture of society as it then was, and to
transfer ourselves back a century or so.

Throughout Ireland at the period we refer to, severe penal
laws were in operation against the Roman Catholics. Irish
Independence had not yet been obtained. The parliament
that then existed was entirely dependent on Westminster.
It could initiate no measure that had not previously been
approved of by the English Privy Council. It was exclu-
sively Protestant, though the Roman Catholics formed seven-
eighths of the population of the country. As law made it
compulsory on the Roman Catholic to go to Protestant
schools if he went to any at all, so law excluded him from
the army, the legal profession and the Houses of Parliament.
In fact the British Constitution tolerated the spectacle of
the whole Roman Catholic population being ostracised from
the British Constitution ! Its benefits were " forbidden
fruit " to them. Looks funny ! Yet it is a sad fact.
Only freeholders and certain leaseholders were entitled
to vote for members of Parliament ; but Roman Catholics
were disqualified from holding freehold, and very few
held under the more favoured lease, and thus were

nearly altogether denied the right even to vote at elections! The Protestant peasant though entitled to vote, had no freedom in his choice. If he refused to vote for his landlord's nominee, eviction was the penalty. In many cases the landlord, for the purpose of swelling his own exchequer, or of cancelling some pressing debts, sold the entire suffrage of his estate to the highest bidder. Here the purchaser might have paid a large sum for the votes of the tenants, but had not the power of evicting them in case they refused to poll for him.

Ireland was governed in this fashion, that seven-eighths of the population was practically denied a vote, and the greater part of the other eighth was to vote under coercion. It was not unnatural that disastrous results would flow from such a policy. To this misgovernment many of the present grievances may be traced; especially the deplorable antagonism that exists between landlord and tenant despite the efforts in the way of remedial legislation made by that eminent statesman, William Ewart Gladstone.

The counties of Mayo and Galway were for years literally torn asunder by the fierce animosities displayed towards one another by the great families residing there. In Mayo, where George Robert first saw the light, and where " darkness quenched his orbs," as Homer would put it, the Binghams, Brownes, Dillons, and Cuffes were the fertile source of feuds. They imported vast crowds of Orangemen from the North to take up the lands from which the Roman Catholic or the stubborn voter had been evicted. With these foreigners they fought out their battles among themselves with varying success and defeat, but in a manner unworthy of a civilised community. Duels and brutal murders were the result of such barbarous tactics, and the morality of those who, in every county must look up for guidance to the representatives of intelligence and influence, became debased and rapidly fell to zero.

## St. Patrick's Day in Castlebar.

In the old Roman Catholic town of Castlebar, or Castle of the Burghs, which was made a borough by James I., and was represented in Parliament by two members as far back as the reign of James II., the 13th Dragoons, under the command of Captain Staples, was stationed. The day for offering the Roman Catholics of the town insult was selected as the 17th of March, and the subject of ridicule was the saint whose name every Irishman the world over has ever held dearest. Ireland at home and abroad was celebrating the feast of her National Saint; the drunken dragoons of the 13th regiment were dishonouring his memory in Castlebar. On the evening of this festival a gang of intoxicated and debauched dragoons staggered down the main street, howling and screeching as they followed an infamous pageant. One ruffian impersonating St. Patrick was decked out in a tattered caubeen, variegated with shamrock and gutter; a frieze swallow-tail full of patches; knee-breeches gartered with suggawns, and a pair of clumsy clogs. His companion was attired in woman's garments; a red flannel petticoat, a faded-looking scrap of a blanket for a shawl, and a cross in his hands : this was to represent Sheelah. In front of the pair strutted a clownish dragoon carrying a bucket of filthy water, which the ruffian who was personating St. Patrick splashed most liberally about by means of a car mop. That blasphemous group paraded the main street of Castlebar on 17th March, perfectly unmolested, and insulted the townsmen who were paralysed both by horror and fear. *O tempora, O mores !* Could those things be done now ?

## Duelling.

At the time we write of, duelling was more prevalent in Ireland than it is at the present day in France, and a thousand times more fatal. The modern Frenchman is excessively sensitive on points of honour, and the most imaginary circumstance will raise his ire and call forth a duel. But this ire which is ever ready to flare up is equally ready to be satisfied. In fact offended honour is now often appeased by a mere exhibition of cutlasses. To draw blood is the exception. But in George Robert's time the duels in Ireland were just as easily provoked, and almost always attended with fatal results. Satisfaction meant death or grievous bodily harm to one of the opponents. The Irish duellists went in for doing business ; the Frenchman of to-day goes in for the glory of the thing without its unpleasant consequences. Everyone in those days, Roman Catholics excepted, was permitted to carry on his person a pistol or sword, often both, and the occasions were frequent when such deadly weapons were appealed to. A breach of etiquette, a witty remark, a sarcastic smile, rivalry in any single pursuit, and most especially where a fair lady was in question, were the never failing causes of duels. In some few instances an apology averted the dangerous encounter, but so reckless of life were they, and so ungoverned were their passions, that a challenge was nearly in every case sent ; if this was rejected or not heeded the offended party administered to the offender a most severe horsewhipping in the most public place.

The powerful families of the day were above the law ; no

one dare check them in their acts of illegality and cruelty. A leader with his strong band of supporters at his back feared neither God nor man, submitted neither to Divine nor human law, dreaded neither civil punishment nor eternal retribution.

This was the composition of society a century and a half ago in the province of Connaught, and in this atmosphere George Robert Fitzgerald was reared. That such a code of morals should influence him in some way would not be wonderful, for a man cannot be expected to live in advance of his time; but that he drank deeply of the unseating morality then prevailing [is only too clearly shown by his lawless career.

## Birth of George Robert Fitzgerald.

George Robert sprang from an illustrious and noble ancestry. It is affirmed that his family can be traced back to that great house of the Guerardi, who were beyond all question noble amongst the noblest in Florence. Some manuscripts discovered in the year 1640, in Lisbon, support this assertion. But there is no need to descend to what may appear to some readers mere fable, in order to prove that the blood that coursed through George Robert's veins was pure and unmixed. Irish History is explicit in this, that the great family of Fitzgerald, which owned Kildare and Desmond, was the stock from which George Robert sprouted. The Fitzgeralds of Desmond and of Kildare came from the Geraldines, who landed in Ireland with Strongbow in the reign of Henry II. of England.

In the middle of the 14th century, about two hundred years after the landing of Strongbow, one Thomas

Fitzgerald, the third son of the first Knight of Kerry, married the daughter and heiress of the Irish chieftain, O'Dea, of Ida, in the county Kilkenny, and in consequence assumed that name, and acquired by this marriage an estate of 1,865 acres, in the barony of Ida, county Kilkenny. The head of the family continued to be known as "The Knight O'Dea" until the sixteenth century, when they resumed the name of Fitzgerald. The Fitzgeralds carried arms under the Royal banner during the famous Civil War that ended in the overthrow of Monarchy, and in the establishment of Republicanism; and shared the same fate as the cause they espoused. Cromwell confiscated their estate of Gurtins, in Kilkenny, and in 1653, transplanted them into Mayo, bestowing on John Fitzgerald a property in Mohinnae, which included the greater part of the parish of Turlough. This grant was confirmed 30th May, 29 Charles II. See "Reported Records of the Commonwealth," Vol. iii., and also Prendergast's "Cromwellian Settlement in Ireland." This John Fitzgerald had a son Thomas, who had George Fitzgerald, the father of George Robert. There is a common error current that John Fitzgerald was of Gurteens or Gorteens, county Waterford. Burke states this, and it is also found on the inscription on the family tomb in Turlough, where the following appears :—" Here lieth the body of Thomas Fitzgerald, "Esqre. He ended a life of as few failings and as many "virtues as ever fell to the share of man, the 15th day of " July, 1747, in the year 86th of his age. He was son and " heir of John Fitzgerald of Gorteen, in the county Water- "ford, where he and his ancestors enjoyed great possessions, "as well as in the county Kilkenny, from the landing of "Strongbow in the reign of King Henry II., A.D. 1111 to "the time of his transplantation to Mayo," and so on . . . Referring to this beautiful monumental stone, erected by George Robert's father, in the abbey close by the old round tower, it was the work of Foys.    In finished sculpture is the Coat of Arms, a boar with a lion rampant and a wreath of shamrocks in the centre, surmounting the inscription, part of which I have given above, reserving the rest for the last chapter.    The entire is surrounded by a border of exquisite tracery.    This skilful sculptist was afterwards poisoned in Italy by a rival.

But the fact is, that John Fitzgerald never owned as much as a sod in county Waterford.    The way the error arose is that John's seat, Gurtins, in county Kilkenny, was near Waterford, and his transplanter's certificate was signed at Waterford by the Commissioners for that neighbourhood. Mr. O'Neill Power is the present proprietor of the said Gurtins, now known as Snow Hill.    The above particulars are correct according to the eminent Irish antiquarian, G. D. Burtchaell, and to my own protracted investigations.

There is no occasion here to comment on that crisis in English History which led to such a revolution in Ireland. It was a happy event on the whole.

A sovereign who thought lightly of trampling under foot the rights of his subjects was brought to the block, and in his stead a military dictator was raised to power.    Charles I. acted on the doctrine of Divine right, which he naturally respected and cherished, having received it from his ances-tors James I. and the Tudors; and he closely adhered to it, finding it to be a convenient and effective way of carrying out his own purposes.

Oliver Cromwell held his power by force of arms; he was respected because he was feared.    A statesman's mind he undoubtedly possessed. He brought into existence an army, the most terrible in war Europe had ever seen. He led it to conquest. He never fought a battle without gaining it. He never gained a battle without annihilating the force opposed to him. Yet, in the long list of outrages that England has authorised in Ireland, in point of cruelty, atrocity, and cold-bloodedness, there is no parallel to those perpetrated by his plundering troops. In the picturesque village of Turlough, about four miles from Castlebar, George Robert was born.

## Turlough some years ago.

It would be exaggeration to talk about the suburbs of this village, or to inquire into the business transacted by its Corporation; there is no electric light, no main drainage, no influenza in this place. And above all, there are no typhoid-generating oysters. Happy spot! The unpretending village is perfectly satisfied with one street, and all the houses, as if by conspiracy, have ranged themselves on one side of it. Some years ago I passes through this village and made the following observations. The extent of commerce gone through there was a barrel of bad mournful-looking porter weekly; strongly resembling ink .to look at, and it was impossibe to put a head on it. A quart or so of extremely vicious whiskey. I am positively certain up to this present moment that a thimbleful would work whole-sale destruction in a regiment of militia men at a thousand yards range. Oh it was powerful! Nitro-glycerine would be mild to it. It would be a good subject for a philosopher to speculate on what became of those poor victims who imbibed it. There were two public-houses entirely. Their

B

appearances were not attractive, but the proprietors made up
for that.   Consumption on the premises was what their faces
at once told you.   They are all gone now I am sure; were they
made of steel inside, they would be molten by this.   There
was also the indispensable forge, which struck one to be a
private house, having nothing about it to suggest that within
was a smith with "large and sinewy hands."   It was far too
respectable looking to be a village forge, and their business
was not overwhelming.   It couldn't be.   Excepting the cur,
the only quadrupeds that used to pass and re-pass were
donkeys and cows.   The former are rather negligent about
shoes, the latter never yet intimated any strong desire to don
these " understandings "!   Yes, there was one old horse—the
village horse !   Very melancholy looking, scraggy, and fairly
variegated with scars.   He was a substitute for a music
organ, for whenever he was put in motion an enchanting
clack-clack air rattled out from his ribs.   A blind man could
see those ribs.   This old veteran, whether it was that more
indulgence was granted to him than otherwise on account
of his being the only one of his species left, or that he ceased
to be what political economists would call a "productive
labourer," certain it is, he too went bare-footed.

After a long day's cycling, I was nearing Turlough when a
nut dropped from my machine.   I soon found it, but
discovered that my wrinch was at home!   Turlough
forge was my only resource, and glad I was at the
moment that such an institution was within a few miles of
me.   Full of the old school-books, the first image my mind
conjured up was " The Smith, a mighty man was he," taken
from that simple, yet charming little poem of Longfellow's.
I expected every village blacksmith was such as the poet
described.   I was prepared to see a massive framed, muscular

looking fellow come out, but *mirabile dictu* a poor old female made her appearance. She was shaking with age, unwashed, shrivelled up and arrayed in rags. She held something like a broken tongs in her trembling hands and proceeded to adjust the machine. She seemed very nervous, and I think made the sign of the cross a few times before coming into close quarters with the strange " Horse." Her efforts were in vain ; indeed the tool was useless for tightening a nut ; after dropping a few coppers, I left Turlough, pushing my bicycle the whole way before me to Castlebar, which I reached with a grim resolve to bring a wrinch the next time I should tour to Turlough. There was also in Turlough— the time I refer to—a police barrack and a post-office.

But what gives Turlough a local fame is the beautiful demesne and splendid mansion of Charles Lionel Fitzgerald. The view that bursts on one just emerging from Turlough on the way to Ballivary, a thriving country village some six miles from Castlebar, is certainly impressive, and has been admired. by every tourist who went that way. Mr. Fitzgerald built the edifice and laid out the demesne ; he resides there and is on good terms with his tenantry for whom he showed great consideration when it was not the fashion to do so. He is Justice of the Peace for the county, and was High Sheriff once. He is known to be generous and courteous, and a man of sterling honour.

## Turlough Castle.

As you emerge from Turlough, with Castlebar on your back, the stately and imposing mansion of the present Fitzgerald bursts on your view. The picture is on your right hand. The splendid cut-stone edifice is planted on an elevation, and as it looks down on an artificial lake enlivened by swans, its tips bathing in the azure sky are delightfully reflected in the calm glassy water beneath. Go visit the scene on a summer's day. A stream stealing languidly from the lake washes the base of an old ruined chapel.

## Pans of Gold !

The story goes that pans of gold were in the bottom of this stream. So many saw the pans glittering in a grigging fashion that divers were brought down from Dublin to take up the pans. But after coming down and approaching the stream no pans were visible. Still several lynx-eyed rustics maintained the pans were there, but could not be raised as they were chained to a rock in the bed of the stream. The river was drained, and the delusion dispelled. Not, however, dispelled completely; for you will yet be told, and don't dare to contradict them, by some old peasants, that the gold is there and is seen at times !

"Still the gold is there !" This recalls to one's mind the persistence of Galileo when imprisoned for maintaining that the earth moved. Everyone then believed the earth to be stationary. Galileo did not, and his constant salutation to every visitor was "*pur e muove*"—"still it moves." Galileo was right ; who knows but that the rustic who persists in the "still the gold is there" is also right ?

Alongside the stream, as we have mentioned above, stands the ruins of an old chapel ; and it is a pleasing sight to see the grey, many-wintered stones entreating support from the interlacing ivy which Nature, coming to the aid of Art, supplied to the crumbling mortar, and to watch the fly-tortured kine taking refuge from the burning rays of a July sun beneath the shades of the venerable ruin.

## Round Tower of Turlough.

On the left, some hundred yards in from the public road, though somewhat obscured by trees, one of the round towers of Ireland shoots erect into the air. The approach to it is a bye-road gradually sloping upwards which leads to the smiling villages of Park and Fisherhill. An observer from the road is disadvantageously located for appreciating the full effect of the building. In height it is nothing remarkable, reaching about 150 feet; it flanks the nave of an old abbey, now roofless. The tower takes its root in the heart of a burial ground where the number of grassy mounds and moss-covered slabs sufficiently indicate the multitude of tenants that sleep there. It was never completed, and the following story is told in relation thereto :—The historic Gubbawn Seer who is credited to have been the architect of every one of these old towers was engaged at this too. Under him an apprentice was working; and by his taste and skill excited the jealousy of the Gubbawn Seer. One day as the two were working away at the top of the tower, a great and bloody battle was taking place a quarter of a mile distant in a field, afterwards called, from that incident, Gurtna-fulla or field of blood. Indeed, this was the exact spot where the cruel murder of one of the chief personages in this sketch, Pat Randal M'Donnel, was perpetrated. Well, all the peasants round flocked to the scene of battle, the Gubbawn and all his workmen too. The apprentice never stirred. His whole attention was engrossed in his work, and he continued finishing most artistically the top of the tower. On the

Gubbawn's return, his envy rising at the beautiful workman-
ship executed by the apprentice, he showed his spite by
taking from the boy the ladder, without which he could not
possibly descend.

Night was approaching, and the young tradesman was
growing afraid and lonesome. At last a passer-by saw the
whole situation, and shrewdly remarked that it was easier to
tumble down two stones than to put up one. The hint was
not lost ; and the boy commenced vigorously throwing down
stone after stone. The news was conveyed to the Gubbawn,
who instantly returned with the ladder, saying, " It
was all a joke," and entreating him to come down and
desist from destroying the beautiful building. As the
apprentice was half way down, the Gubbawn gave the
ladder a sudden jerk, throwing the boy a lifeless mass against
the ground. It was never completed. The Government
some few years ago authorised committees to look after the
round towers which were decaying away, and thus many of
them, the Turlough one included, were saved from dissolu-
tion.

These round towers, 118 of which are in Ireland at present,
were the subject of endless conjecture and speculation among
antiquarians who connected them with Pagan times and
Pagan rites. Dr. Petrie has, however, settled the matter
in showing that they were built by Christian architects and
for religious purposes. Their date is sometime between the
sixth and ninth centuries.

Such was Turlough some years ago ; the author paid a
later visit to the village and noted much improvement and
more prosperity. To-day it presents the appearance of a
neat, cleanly, snug village, and gives hopes of further advance
in prosperity and comfort.

## George Robert's Parents.

George Robert was born in his father's house, a building of remarkable taste. It occupied the site now filled by the capacious stables of the present Fitzgerald. His father's name was George, and he had two sons, the eldest being George Robert, the subject of this sketch; the second being Charles Lionel. His mother was Lady Hervey, sister to the Earl of Bristol, the Bishop of Derry of volunteer celebrity. She died in the year 1753, when George Robert was at an age when a mother's watchful eye and kind correction are most valuable. After her death George Fitzgerald lived a worthless and selfish life with a mistress. This conduct chilled the warm feelings that his son George Robert would naturally have had for him; for now the memory of the loving wife and fond mother whose spirit had flown to a brighter and happier region, was disgraced. The affection a child shares with his father and mother when alive, is after the death of either solely centred in the surviving parent. Most surviving parents know this; 'tis common; but it was not George Fitzgerald's lot. For the immoral and ungrateful act of treating his true wife's memory so badly alienated all the sentiments of affection his eldest son was capable of having.

George Robert, at a very early age, exhibited features of character strikingly adapted for the army; he moreover expressed a strong desire to join that profession. Indeed it is likely he inherited this *penchant* from his father, who had been a very distinguished captain in the Austrian army. He was, however, as yet too young, and in addition required some schooling.

## George Robert at College.

To Eton George Robert was sent, and there passed four years in the study of polite literature, and in the pursuit of physical games.   English literature, French plays, and Latin verse fascinated him ; while his recreation hours were given to athletics, in which he acquired the reputation of being the fleetest runner and best jumper in the school.   The last year of his collegiate course, he was leader of a band of twenty sworn chums, and with this organised body he was the terror not only of the students, but even of the professors and deans.   He left Eton a polished, refined young gentleman ; his body evenly developed and graceful.   Eton was then the nursery for the scions of the aristocratic families of Great Britain.   Among schools, it reached the highest rung of the social ladder.

At the age of seventeen he bid farewell to Eton and entered the army : he was quartered in Galway, and here his duels began.   Their history will occupy the next chapter.

## CHAPTER II.

Galway duels with Cæsar French and with Colonel Thompson—In France. A. H. Rowan, Major Baggs, " Steel Waistcoat."—His First Marriage—The Volunteers—Lord Norbury—Lord Clare— The Brownes and the Binghams—Fatal duel at Greenhills—Prosecution and Escape—Sligo—Duel in Castlebar with Martin—The Mayo Cock vanquishes the Galway Cock—His Second Marriage— George Browne of Brownestown.

# Fitzgerald's Duels in Galway, Mayo, and —— on the Continent.

WE have already mentioned that George Robert's father was for some years a captain in the Austrian army, and from this fact it was clear that the son would meet with no great opposition in making the same mode of life the profession of his choice. In fact his father's sympathies and prejudices ran in that direction, and encouraged rather than disapproved of the move George Robert had decided on. He was scarcely six months out of Eton when his father purchased for him a commission in the army, a practice abolished since 1871, on the advice of Mr. Gladstone. He took up quarters in Galway. By his natural gifts, as well as by his acquired ones, George Robert was extremely well qualified to be a great favourite with the fair sex. His elegant manners, his winning address, his pleasing features were backed up by a well shaped and daintily attired person. His clear cut features, middle sized athletic frame were soon known to nearly all the young ladies of the town, and it is needless to say there was no scarcity of interesting girls in the " Citie of the Tribes " to make such an innocent amusement as a flirtation pleasant and lively.

On one occasion George Robert was so overcome by the charming beauty of a little milliner with whom he was just beginning to flirt, that he jumped the counter, and *vi et armis* snatched a kiss. The frightened damsel gave a shriek which at once brought on the scene a sturdy, self-opinionated shop-keeper from the opposite side of the street. This man, Lynch, never saw anything in lovely woman worthy of man's affections; he had lived a soured old bachelor up to this, and died one too. But on this occasion he grew all at once chivalrous, rushed across the street; darted into the draper's shop; flared up, and boiling over with virtuous indignation began to " ballyrag " the offender. He hadn't gone very far, however, in his litany of compliments when George Robert seized a roll of calico and almost made the excited town-councillor swallow the dose. He literally corked his mouth with a plug of glazed calico. Lynch at once challenged George Robert, who replied, " I'll not draw swords with a boorish shopkeeper; bring me a gentleman and I'll promise you I'll meet him." Lynch left the shop, and the first person he met was Cæsar French.

## Duel with Cæsar French.

French was a Galway gentleman, and sometime after a Receiver over Turlough estate, and empowered by old Fitzgerald to keep a strict eye on George Robert. Mr. Lynch briefly informed French of the occurrence and asked him to fight Fitzgerald; this he agreed to. Both combatants retired to a small back room in the draper's shop, locked the door and presented pistols. They were eighteen feet apart; French gave the signal; both fired. George Robert's bullet grazed French's right temple; French's pistol did not go off. Fitzgerald gallantly offered his powder-horn to his opponent to prime his weapon better, and proposed to renew the combat. As they were in the act of doing so, the fragile door was burst open by a crowd of people who had just heard of the affair, and the combatants were separated. This incident put a stop to Fitzgerald's career of flirtation in Galway. But strange to say, on the next day he was in another duel which nearly terminated in his death. The escape was miraculous; the duel was with a brother officer, Colonel Thompson.

## Duel with Colonel Thompson.

The night of the above encounter with Cæsar French, nothing was talked of in barracks but "Fitzgerald" and the "Milliner." It was the sole topic of conversation and Fitzgerald did not altogether like the publicity of the affair. Some of the officers quizzed and bantered him over it; some declared he behaved manfully towards the crack-shot French; one officer who was always, to the disgust of George Robert, parading his family rank, and informing every one that nothing but the purest blood flowed in his veins, offended Fitzgerald so keenly that a duel was the result. This officer, Colonel Thompson by name, said in the presence of Fitzgerald that the whole proceedings was dishonourable and cowardly. "Do you charge me with cowardice, Thompson?" asked George Robert. "I do most certainly," answered Thompson, "and had I been Lynch, I'd have horsewhipped you through the streets of Galway, and after that got a gentleman who would meet you with pistols." "Mine Honour!" cried Fitzgerald in a rage, "if you don't meet me to-morrrow and pay dearly for your swaggering." The officers cheered Fitzgerald, who was very popular with them, both on account of his quick sense of honour and his reckless "dash," of character. They fought next day, when Thompson received a wound in the hand, and Fitzgerald was hit in the temple, knocking him over groaning in a pool of blood !  It was a bad hit.  A surgeon was brought from Dublin to attend him, and after a delicate and most skilful operation extracted the bullet.  Six months elapsed before George Robert was able to walk abroad, and even then he was very weak.

From this wound we may trace the symptoms of eccentricity, if not of insanity, which colour his after career.  The brain suffered so much from the effects of the wound, that the giddiness, impetuosity, and want of prudence exhibited by him till his death, cannot be wondered at.  On his recovery he set out for Turlough, and spent a few months in his father's house ; but life was so dull and slow in such a place that he soon exchanged it for the gaiest city in the world, Paris.

## George Robert's Duels in France.

George Robert directed his steps towards France, and soon earned for himself there the reputation of being a noted duellist.  This accomplishment, together with his good breeding and elegant manners, secured for him, in a very short time, favour at the Court of Louis XV.

A. Hamilton Rowan in his "Autobiography" tells us he met Fitzgerald at Fontainbleau, and that his fame as a duellist was established there, and that his influence in Court was very considerable.

Rowan was selling a race-horse which he had brought with him from England.  George Robert purchased it for a hundred guineas and gave Rowan a cheque for the amount. On presenting the cheque to George Robert's banker, the latter apologised and said he could not give cash for it. Rowan sent back the cheque to Fitzgerald, stating he would take back the horse as he heard the animal did not suit. This affair, instead of being the cause of a duel, as Rowan greatly feared, was the occasion of a very polite letter from George Robert begging to be excused for his cheque being dishonoured, and requesting Rowan to let him know when he intended to sell the horse again.

The next time A. Hamilton Rowan met George Robert was one evening leaving a theatre in Paris. Mr. Rowan had invited to supper a few friends who were at the play with him, and meeting an old acquaintance, Captain Williamson, in the company of George Robert, asked them both to join the party. As they were all coming out of the theatre, George Robert accosted a gentleman, quite a stranger to the rest of them; he was a Major Baggs. " I hear, sir," said George Robert, " that you report I owe you three hundred pounds, and that you can't get it from me ? " " Yes, and more," returned Baggs. Some hot words were interchanged which resulted in Fitzgerald insisting on having the matter decided at once with swords ; Baggs refused, but said he would fight him next day with pistols, and in a " clock-case " if he pleased ! George Robert flung his glove in the Major's face, stepped into Rowan's carriage and drove to the hotel.

Two days passed by, and no word of Baggs. On the third day Rowan met Baggs at an opera, and the subject talked of was Fitzgerald's insult a few nights previous. Baggs told some Frenchmen in his company that Fitzgerald ran off in disguise, and fled the country.

This Rowan denied and quitted the company of the boasting Major.

## Famous Duel with Major Baggs.

Next morning a messenger came from Baggs to Fitzgerald inquiring was he ready; the latter replied in the affirmative, and the combatants met at noon in a spacious field in the open country, far from the ken of anyone. The place selected was on Austrian soil, as there were certain chances of being detected on French territory. There was some dispute as to the nature of the weapons to be used: Fitzgerald was insisting on swords as well as a brace of pistols; the Major was not even so modest in his requirements—nothing less than arm-chairs, flasks of powder, and bags of bullets being the order! It was finally agreed to do with a brace of pistols each. As Fitzgerald's second took ill at the last moment, he entreated Rowan to act instead, and got his consent. At the appointed time the duellists took their places, eight paces apart, a pistol in each hand. On the signal being about to be given, Baggs cried out "time," and charged George Robert with being *plastronné*, meaning he was lined with a steel waistcoat. Fitzgerald at once refuted the accusation by stripping, and in turn requested Baggs to do likewise; but the latter, pleading the coldness of the air, was excused. The Major sank back on his haunches like a cat about to spring; Fitzgerald leaned forward as if he was making a lounge, both fired, and were just raising the second pistols when Baggs shouted, "I'm wounded." "But you're not dead," cried Fitzgerald, letting him have the second pistol in the thigh. With that, Baggs jumped up as if gaining new strength, rushed at Fitzgerald, who ran off. The chase across the field lasted a few minutes;

Fitzgerald flung his empty pistol in the Major's face, whereupon the latter discharged the contents of his second pistol in George Robert's leg, bringing him down at once. Baggs, from this exertion, which was supported by unnatural strength, became completely exhausted, and fell down flat, bleeding profusely from the wound he had received above the knee. After a moment or two Fitzgerald rose, returned to his opponent and said, "We are both wounded, let us go back and see this out." The poor Major did not respond to the invitation; he was extremely weak, and had to be carried off to a surgeon, while Fitzgerald went off with Rowan, not much the worse of the encounter.

News of the affair spread fast, and reached the governor of the province, whereupon he ordered all concerned in it to be brought before him at Valenciennes. Rowan undertook to explain all, and after some conversation the governor remarked, "But, Sir, the first time you came to me I think I saw something on your watch-chain like a mosaic jewel; are you a brother?" Rowan told him he was; that he had been initiated in Cambridge, and was master of that Lodge. This bit of information exculpated them all, and the entire party got off scot-free. George Robert now returned to Turlough, and conceived the happy idea of matrimony. Most of us have to go through that; and certain it is if our parents had not done the same, neither you, dear reader, nor my humble self, would now be enjoying the advantages of this nineteenth century.

## George Robert's First Marriage.

He became acquainted with a Miss Conolly, daughter of Mr. Conolly, of Castletown, county Kildare. Her connections were of the highest stamp. She was sister-in-law to the Earl of Buckingham, then Viceroy of Ireland. Their intimacy, however, soon ripened into love, and love terminated in a secret promise to marriage. Her friends did not at all countenance the addresses George Robert was paying, and would not for an instant hear of a union between them. During the courtship George Robert lived on an exceedingly grand scale—after the fashion of an Eastern prince, in fact. No money, no exertion was spared to make him appear the greatest nobleman in the west of Ireland. He kept twelve first-rate hunters, and a retinue of liveried servants. He used to ride through the main street of Castlebar dressed gorgeously in broad-cloth trimmed with deep gold lace. His spurs and stirrup-irons were of solid silver, while his full-blooded steed was bitted and shod with the same precious metal. He was at all times accompanied by a dozen practised shots mounted on spirited horses, and arrayed in brilliant costumes. The fact is well known that on many occasions he flung around indiscriminately handfulls of sixpences as he paraded in state the streets of the county town. This extravagance and display continued unchecked while he was paying his addresses to Miss Conolly. One evening he rode to her house, and after spending about an hour there, he took her up secretly on his horse, and bore her off in the real Lochinvar fashion. The iron front-gate was locked, but the couple cleared it in a spring and drew no rein for twelve miles, when they reached a small inn and spent the night there. Next morning they left for Paris ; there the marriage was solemnized and the honeymoon enjoyed. During their pleasant stay in Paris they were introduced to some of the noblest in the Court of Louis XV. When a good part of the money Miss Conolly had with her, being left some by a friend, was spent, the happy couple returned to Ireland, took a house in Upper Merrion Square, Dublin, number twenty-three, and passed some years between this residence and Turlough. How Miss Conolly disappeared from her father's home was enshrouded in a dark mystery, but the porter found two silver shoes which had been stripped going over the gate, and this let in the light on the whole affair.

## The Volunteers!

About this time the Irish Volunteers sprang into existence. A noble and immortal body! Great Britain was carrying on a deadly struggle with France, Spain, and the revolted colonies in America. The north of Ireland was coasted by pirates, and the black flag was threatening Belfast city. Paul Jones had Ireland in a state of trepidation. The citizens indeed applied to the Government for aid, but only half a troop of horse and half a troop of infantry was sent. Thus the Irish had to fall back on themselves for defencè, and the body that rose into arms for the protection of their country from the pirate scourge was the Irish Volunteers. In every parish men were enlisted; recruits drilled, supplied with arms, horses, and artillery. Organisation was perfect throughout the length and breadth of the land. In 1780, when Henry Grattan declared that "no power on earth save the King, Lords, and Commons of Ireland had a right to make laws for Ireland," the Volunteers formed the standing force of the country. George Robert joined that body, and rode on a little pony from Dublin to Castlebar, one hundred and twenty-six Irish miles, to contest the Colonelcy of the Mayo Legion, made vacant by the retirement of Lord Lucan. He was, however, defeated; a man named Pat Randal McDonnel being elected.

C

## The "Brownes and the Binghams" Duel.

George Robert cherished an intense hatred towards the Browne family. The member of that family who was Fitzgerald's greatest enemy was the Right Hon. Denis Browne, brother of the third Earl of Altamount. Denis Browne in in his early days was a very handsome and extremely well-built man. He married a sister of Sir Ross Mahon's, and after that lived a careless, indolent life. He grew lazy, corpulent, and gluttonous, and his temper became violent and passionate. In the elections for the county of Mayo the Binghams and Brownes were rivals, and enmities of the deepest dye grew up between them. James Bingham, Lord Clanmorris, came forward as a candidate for the county at the time we are writing of, and Denis Browne, only then twenty-three years of age, opposed him. James Browne, Prime Sergeant, and uncle to Denis Browne, told him he should fight Bingham. Denis met Bingham on the steps of the Courthouse in Castlebar, jostled him with his shoulder, and threw him on the street in the mud. Bingham challenged Browne, and both fought for fully thirty minutes in the horse-barracks before crowds of electors who had come in to vote. Browne vanquished Bingham, and thus won the applause as well as the votes of the electors, and was returned at the head of the poll. Denis Browne could do what he liked in Mayo for thirty years. He was an absolute dictator there. Lord Clare conferred on him all honours, and gave him unlimited authority. He could liberate any prisoner he wished, and give titles and pensions to any one he cared about. In the year 1806 the Whigs came into power, and Ponsonby was Lord Lieutenant for Ireland. This change affected Denis Browne ; it put an end to his importance and cut short his career of despotism. The year 1828 records his demise.

## George Robert and the Brownes.

George Robert was now, as we have said, renting a beautiful house in Dublin. During his stay there he on one occasion fired at Denis Browne ; on another had a duel with Toler, afterwards Chief Justice of the Common Pleas, better known in Irish history as the infamous Norbury. At a Levee in Dublin Castle Fitzgibbon, afterwards Lord Clare, had some altercation with Fitzgerald when the latter, before the entire company, actually spat in his face, an affront never forgotten by Fitzgibbon. This was the way George Robert conducted himself in the city.

But, not content with insulting the aristocrats of Dublin, he proceeds to Westport, and there grossly affronts the Brownes. He went to their magnificent mansion in Westport, and demanded admission in a haughty tone. He wished to see their fine " wolf-dog." This animal was highly prized by his master, and was honoured with the name " Prime Sergeant, " after Lord Altamount, James Browne, brother to the then Lord Sligo. The Prime Sergeant was a big, fat, dull, heavy bruiser of a fellow. But he was the " great lawyer " of the family, and superstitious veneration was paid to every syllable that fell from his lips on a legal subject. When Fitzgerald was brought before the muchly-prized wolf-dog he carelessly drew his pistol and pierced the brute through. It was a carcase in a moment. He commanded the servants to tell their master that "until the noble peer became more charitable to the wandering poor and allowed the starving creatures to get some of the bones and meat which the glutton of a wolf-dog swelled himself with he could not tolerate such animals. " And, showing how considerate he was, he left a note to the effect that he would, however, permit Lady Anne, Lady Elizabeth, and Lady Charlotte to keep one lap-dog each. He then strutted through Westport, jubilantly proclaiming that he had shot the " Prime Sergeant." This provoked great excitement in the town, and the authorities were about to arrest him for the murder of Counsellor Browne, when he dispelled the illusion by informing them that he shot " a much worthier animal, the big wolf-dog!" Indeed, Fitzgerald was by no means a favourite with the people of Westport ; and on this occasion he found matters becoming so hot that he had to make a hasty retreat.

## Richard Martin : Fatal Duel.

Richard Martin came from a most respectable Galway family who lived in Ballinahinch. In 1779 he joined the Connaught Bar, and, in addition to his title of Barrister-at-Law, he soon acquired that of Colonel of the Galway Volunteers. He was known both as Counsellor Martin and Colonel Martin. Richard Martin's intimate friends were James O'Hara, Recorder of Galway and Grenadier Captain in the Galway Volunteers, and a James Jordan, of Rosslevin Castle. The latter was one of the most intellectual and sociable of the Jordans of Rosslevin. Oliver Burke relates all this in his " Connaught Circuit," a work very entertaining and very well written, but inaccurate as to some facts and many places. An old but esteemed member of the Connaught Bar, now in his grave, furnished me ample grounds for such a criticism.

James Jordan and Richard Martin travelled the continent

together. They visited America and Jamaica, and on their return fell out at a Bar-dinner. They both were dining with the other members of the Connaught Bar, during the Castlebar Assizes, when Martin reproached Jordan before all the barristers, with unkind treatment of his mother. Jordan challenged Martin to a duel, but the latter being one of the best shots in the province of Connaught, refused to accept the challenge. Jordan insisted on the duel, and Greenhills, a spot about three miles from Castlebar, on the road to Westport, was chosen. The duel came off, and Jordan was fatally wounded by a bullet in the groin ; he was taken into Mr. Bourke's, a Justice of the Peace, who lived in Greenhills House at the time, and after a day's intense agony, succumbed to the effects of the wound. Richard Martin is described by A. H. Ronan, who knew him well, as a man who displayed "urbanity towards women, benevolence towards men ; humanity towards the brute creatiqn ; he was very charitable ; had no politics ; was well accomplished." Martin represented Galway in the Irish Parliament, and his son later on filled the same position.

## Martin Prosecutes George Robert for Illtreating his Father.

Martin was on terms of the closest intimacy with the Brownes, and any insult offered to them was painful and irritating to him. Fitzgerald's insolence to the Westport family annoyed Martin exceedingly, and certainly formed one of the sources of the animosity he entertained towards Fitzgerald. Another reason for the ill-feeling between those two gentlemen, was this : In 1782, Martin was engaged as counsel by George Fitzgerald the father, and Charles Lionel the younger son in prosecuting George Robert for ill-treating

his father. It came about this way. Old Fitzgerald had
obtained from the Lord Chancellor a writ for the arrest of
his son. Under this authority, the father and Charles
Lionel attempted to seize George Robert in the Grand Jury
room during the Ballinrobe Summer Assizes, but failed, for
the offender escaped and fled to Turlough. When the
father reached home he encountered his undutiful son, and
threatened to deprive him of his " fee." This was something
considerable, as George Robert was to receive an " estate
in tale male " of the father's property, on the decease
of that person ; in simpler language, George Robert
was, on the death of his father, to own Turlough estate
for life, and on his own death, his eldest son was to suc-
ceed ; if he had no son, Charles Lionel was to come next.
In addition to this, old Fitzgerald had promised to give
£1,000 annually, during his own lifetime, to George Robert,
a promise never adequately fulfilled, and hence a cause of
many quarrels between the father and son. This threat
of the father angered George Robert greatly, and urged him
on to the unnatural crimes, for which he was soon imprisoned.
The way George Robert met the threats of his father was
by imprisoning him in a grotto in Turlough, over which
there were inscribed some choice classical quotations. At
the Castlebar Spring Assizes, 1783, " true bills " were found
against George Robert ; he applied for a postponement, but
was refused. The prosecution was for imprisoning his
father ; for putting a chain on him ; and for making him
pull a dray. An affidavit was read stating that the father
was not confined. Martin said that the best proof would be
the attendance of the father at the next Commission of the
Peace for the county Mayo. Lenon was engaged in defend-
ing George Robert, and remarked that the father was one

of the worst men living, and that it would only be right to confine such a public nuisance. He applied for a postponement.

Martin opposed vehemently a postponement, and concluded thus: "Though I believe that in the course of a long life this wretched father has committed many crimes, yet the greatest crime against society and the blackest sin against Heaven he ever perpetrated, is the having begotten the traverser." George Robert heard this, and said aloud in the Court, with a bitter smile: "Martin, you look very healthy now; you take good care of your constitution; but I tell you, this day you have taken very bad care of your life." It was proved that George Robert chained his father to a dray; that he sometimes tied him to a muzzled bear! Lord Hugh Carleton sentenced him to three years, and to a fine of £500 to the King. Indeed the jury did not take two minutes coming to a verdict. The Attorney-General was the Right Hon. Barry Yelverton.

## Imprisonment—Escape.

Fitzgerald was just four days in Castlebar Prison when he escaped. He scattered a bag of silver and gold on the floor, and the warders were so busily engaged in scrambling for and pocketing the bright coins, that our hero made off.

He was pursued to Sligo by Pat Randal McDonnel at the head of the Castlebar Volunteer corps. A reward of £300 was offered for his arrest. Not till two days had passed was he caught. The Town Mayor of Sligo, a Mr. M'Hall, seized him, and he was sent off to Newgate. Here he spent six months, at the end of which time his health began to give way. Through the influence of Conolly, his father-in-law, who was related to the Viceroy, Duke of Buckingham, he was released.

It was during this imprisonment he composed the famous appeal, a production cleverly written indeed, and part of which I shall re-produce when his history is told. Charles Lionel Fitzgerald took advantage of his brother's absence by getting possession of the house and demesne in Turlough; and most of George Robert's desperadoes were enlisted for the Indian service by Jonah Barrington who at that time was spending some days in the west of Mayo recruiting. On coming out of prison, the sad news of the death of his beloved wife reached George Robert. He hastened to Turlough to have a long look at her before the chill earth should close for ever over her remains.

He was a good husband to her, and loved her with all the force his passionate soul was capable of ; her death deeply grieved him. She left one child, a beautiful little girl ; of her the Conollys took charge. The remains were brought from Turlough to Celbridge, a small village quite near Maynooth, and there interred. George Robert's ill-feeling towards Martin grew every day more intense, and occasioned two duels, the first of which occurred in this way :—

## Duel between George Robert and Martin.

One night Mrs. Crawford was playing " Belvidera " in Crowe Street Theatre, Dublin, before a crowded audience. Martin was sitting in a box in the front row just near the stage, when he heard from behind a noisy foot-step, and a sharp hasty command to open the door of the box. He looked back and observed George Robert very angry looking, making his way into the box immediately behind him. Martin left it and came alongside Fitzgerald merely for the sake of company; the latter stared him fixedly for a few moments, then burst out laughing in his face. " Have you anything particular to say to me, Fitzgerald ? " asked Martin. " Only to tell you I followed you from Castlebar to proclaim you the bully of the Altamounts," replied Fitzgerald defiantly. "You have said enough, Mr. Fitzgerald ; you no doubt expect to hear from me, and it shall be early in the morning," said Martin. " I shall hear from you ! " replied Fitzgerald contemptuously; "this will refresh your memory then," hitting Martin a blow in the eyes with his glove. He then left the theatre. Martin a few days later met a young fellow named George Lyster, a cousin of George Robert's, and asked him to deliver a message to Fitzgerald, appointing the time and particulars of the coming duel. On Lyster communicating the message to George Robert, the latter grew indignant, seized his cudgel which was decorated with green ribbon, and saying, " How dare you, you young upstart, bring such a message to me ? " made a few blows at Lyster breaking a beautiful diamond ring that was on his little finger, and dislocating the joint of his middle finger. He was in the act of thrashing the " soul " out of him, when the uproar drew the attention of the police, and both were brought before Mr. Justice Robinson. Lyster's story was not believed; George Robert said Lyster asked him to fight Martin ; he refused, then Lyster set about beating him, till the alarm given attracted the police. Lyster was returned for trial and Fitzgerald bound to prosecute. As there was no meeting between Fitzgerald and Martin this time, the latter became more eager than ever to chastise his enemy.

Very soon after this, both chanced to be in Castlebar.

Martin was staying in Lord Lucan's residence awaiting Lord Altamount's carriage which was coming from Westport. Fitzgerald was doing the "braggadocio" in the town parading up and down the streets and swearing he would stop the carriage. "For though the horse is a brave animal, I fancy Altamount's horses are like their master, and cannot stand the smell of powder," said George Robert. Martin on hearing this boasting, emerged from the house, and with two holster pistols he sauntered down the town, linking Dr. Merlin. They came up to Fitzgerald who was with Fenton, a crack duellist, at Potter Finch's, a public-house, just about the middle of the main street on the west side. Martin ordered Fitzgerald to draw swords at once; Fitzgerald refused, saying the pavement was so bad that it would hurt his hip, which had not recovered fully from the wounds he received in his duels on the Continent. Martin then said, " I'm going to the Barrack-yard, where you'll have even ground, and I expect you there, sir." " I'll consult my own leisure, and be in no hurry; after striking you in the theatre the other night for your pertness, and you letting it pass, you haven't the pluck of a worm," said Fitzgerald. Martin made a quick stroke at him with a switch, but Fitzgerald parried it. There was a large crowd now surrounding the four notables, and most of the feeling ran in favour of Martin, for Fitzgerald became unpopular through his reckless and bullying conduct. After just warding off the blow aimed at him : "The Mayo cock against the Galway cock any day; come, Martin, for £100, and damn me if I don't stretch you!" cried Fitzgerald. "Make it ten times the amount and I'll meet you," replied Martin. Both, accompanied by their seconds, walked down the town to Barrack Street.

This is a small street turning off to the left as one goes up Rush Street.  People are yet alive in Castlebar who remember seeing a revenue police-station at the corner of Barrack Street; those police were occupied in still-hunting. Well, in Barrack Street there was a horse-barrack, and to this place the duellists retired.  Sentries were placed at the gate to keep out the crowds who were eager to be observers of the combat.  Martin, leaning up against the barrack, took his position twelve paces distant from Fitzgerald.  " Ah sir, come closer," said Fitzgerald ; " this is child's play ; a cannon ball wouldn't reach you at that distance off.  Are you afraid you'll be hurt ? "  Martin said, " I'll come as close as you please, for I'll march up till I lay my pistol on your face."  They both advanced till their pistols were touching ! On the word being given, both pulled their triggers; Fitzgerald was jerked back and fell forcibly on his side, completely dazed ; Martin remained in his position, untouched ; his bullet had met Fitzgerald on the breast, but striking one of the large silver buttons in his coat, bounded off, doing him no serious injury.  Fitzgerald's pistol did not go off at all.  Martin, seeing his opponent down and apparently dying, was pulling out a second pistol to put an end to his greatest enemy, when Fitzgerald, recovering himself, cried out, " Honour, Martin, Honour ! where's your spirit?" Martin replied, "If you're not disabled I'll wait as long as you choose ; come, be quick."  George Robert rose up, took his place : now, ten feet apart : both fired, and both hit. "Struck for £1,000," shouted Fitzgerald, as Martin tumbled down ; he was severely wounded in the breast, where the ball lodged.  Fitzgerald narrowly escaped ; the ball whizzed by his neck, carrying away some of the skin.  Martin bled profusely on the ground, and his friends were greatly en-

raged ; the cheering of the Castlebar boys outside for
Fitzgerald, who entirely won them over all of a sudden,
set the Martin faction furious. "Don't stir, Fitzgerald,"
roared Dr. Merlin, Martin's second, "you'll stand my blaze
too." "Let glister-pipe come on," said Fitzgerald ; "I've
game blood in me yet ; don't think that Mayo will lie down
for Galway." The cheers and applause from the outside
audience had made George Robert so brave that he would
have faced a raging lion. Fitzgerald's second, Fenton, in-
terfered, and wheeling George Robert off, said, " No, no,
Merlin ; one at a time is enough." George Robert went
over to the wounded Martin, shook hands, saying, "The
Altamounts are the whole cause of this." On leaving the
barrack, the crowd seized him, and huzzaing and cheering,
carried him on their shoulders up the whole main street.
Martin was brought to the residence of the county surgeon,
Dr. Lindsay, where the ball was extracted. Fitzgerald
called a few times to visit Martin during his recovery, and
acted very nobly all through the affair.

## George Robert's Second Marriage.

Miss Vaughan, of Carramore, near Ballinrobe, now became the object of Fitzgerald's affections, and very soon
his companion for weal or for woe. During their married
life they were very much attached to each other. They
settled down in Turlough House, and lived very happily
together.

## George Robert and George Browne of Brownstown.

There is a pleasant anecdote which I heard from one
who had it from the lips of a person then alive ; and it is this:

Fitzgerald bought a horse from Mrs. Browne of Brownstown, and did not pay for it, though frequently reminded by letters. The eldest son, George, grandfather of George Browne, once member for Mayo, was a good, affable gentleman, and a practical Catholic. Annoyed at Fitzgerald's coolness and indifference, he mounted one of his best steeds, rode in fury to Fitzgerald's house, and knocked "loud and long" at the hall-door. The servant came out and inquired what he wanted. "I wish to see Fitzgerald," replied George Browne. Fitzgerald came down, ordered his horse to be stabled, and invited him cordially inside. Both took seats in the front room, and chatted away in a friendly manner while they were discussing a bottle of sparkling champagne. The question of paying for the horse came on, and Fitzgerald began by saying the animal wasn't satisfactory, and that he wasn't sure he would keep him.

They soon strolled out to the garden, and walked leisurely round a path which encircled a solitary tree. This tree was all perforated with holes made by an auger, and stood twenty yards from the box-wood of the circular path. They were chatting away, when all of a sudden Fitzgerald drew his revolver and sent a bullet clean through one of the holes. "That's a nice thing," said George Robert, walking on. As soon as they had come round to the same spot, Browne drew his revolver and pierced the same hole through. "That's not bad," remarked Browne. Fitzgerald picked up a small nail off the ground; fixed it loosely in the bark of the tree, and fired. He hit it fair on the head, burying it in the trunk of the tree. "Now Browne, for you; there's something to be proud of," said Fitzgerald. They continued walking round, till Browne took

a pin from his waistcoat, put it in the bark, fired, and sunk
it into he tree. " Come in, Browne," exclaimed Fitzgerald;
and on entering the room, Fitz-erald took from his safe
a bundle of notes and handed them to Browne, saying:
" Here's treble the price of your horse, and good-bye."

Browne departed satisfied, and George Robert felt
himself humbled at meeting his equal with a revolver.   It
is related that this George Browne was the best shot by
far in Ireland ; that in England, France, and America, he
fought many duels, and was never hurt, but always hit his
man ; that as a marksman he had never met his match.   In
fact, he was feared by every one all about the country.   On
one occasion he sheltered a priest who was under a warrant
of arrest ; the soldiers searched all Hollymount, Kiltimagh,
and Brownstown for him, and finally came to Browne's house
and demanded the clergyman, producing a warrant signed
by Denis Browne, J.P.   George Browne promised to bring
the priest to the courthouse, so both went to the Clare-
morris courthouse, and in the presence of all G. Browne
pulled out two big bull-dogs and threw them on the
"green table" before Denis Browne, saying: "On your
knees, sir, and swear to God you'll never sign a warrant for
a priest again ; or by heavens you'll have to take up one of
these pistols and play with me for a few moments."   Down
went Denis on his knees, and swore the oath.

We have now to relate the chief episode in the eventful
life of Fitzgerald ; and are sorry to say that it is of a rather
deplorable character.   The episode terminated in bringing
George Robert Fitzgerald, a gentleman of high birth, refined
manners, polished education, and generous heart, to an
ignominious death—execution by the common hangman.
How this came about will be see in the next chapters.

# CHAPTER III.

Pat Randal McDonnel—Love Affair—Miss Anne O'Donel's Abduction—Pontoon—The Assizes' Judges are attacked after leaving Castlebar—Murder of Pat Randal McDonnel—George Robert in Castlebar Prison.

## George Robert and Pat Randal McDonnel.

IF the introduction of Pat Randal McDonnel to our readers involves us in details regarding his life, we shall offer no apology, for he constitutes the central figure of a group of characters who are to remain on the stage till the last scene of this eventful drama closes.

Pat Randal McDonnel was the son of a Roman Catholic gentleman, Alexander McDonnel, who lived in Chancery Hall, county Mayo. His father led a life of vice and sloth, and it soon became apparent that the son would turn out a faithful copy of the parent. Of this he gave early promise, for at the age of fourteen, he was expelled from his father's house for disgraceful and dishonourable conduct. His maternal uncle, Patrick Fitzgerald, a solicitor in Castlebar, received the outcast into his office and made him a member of the profession. After two years his paternal uncle died, leaving him a large legacy by will. He bequeathed to him the entire property of Chancery Hall, a name it derived from the following incident :—

The uncle when alive repeatedly promised Pat Randal that he would make provision for him in his will. So on the decease of that gentleman, Pat Randal naturally made inquiries concerning the mysterious will ; after much worry, he discovered that it was in the possession of his father. One night he stole the will from where it was concealed. The father swore informations against him for having burglariously broken into his house; the trial came off at Ballinrobe Assizes, 1778, and resulted in the acquittal of Pat Randal. The will was produced, declaring the entire property to be Pat Randal's. He then filed a bill against the purchaser of the property (Pat Randal's father having sold it) for knowingly buying it under fraudulent circumstances, and the Lord Chancellor issued a decree putting him in possession. The property received the name Chancery Hall from the amount of litigation it was the subject of. The place is about a quarter of a mile from Turlough.

## Love Affair; Miss Anne O'Donel.

Miss Anne O'Donel, of Mossvale or Moynafallen, had two suitors, Hyacinth Martin and Timothy Brecknock. The former was a member of the Mayo Volunteer corps, a great friend of Pat Randal's, and closely related to Colonel Martin, whom we have seen duelling with Fitzgerald. Between the latter and Hyacinth Martin there was no friendship lost; indeed it was not likely that they should be anything but foes. Brecknock, however, was a bosom friend of George Robert's, and as the latter had great influence with old O'Donel it was likely Martin would be completely "out of the running."

Brecknock was educated in Jesus College, Oxford, and a member of the English Bar. He entertained a supreme contempt for Roman Catholics. He was old and wicked looking. It was said of him that he wore the gallows in his face. Indeed we have it on fairly reliable authority that he was the reputed son of Bishop of Landaff.

Miss O'Donel certainly liked Martin's personal appearance, his connection ; but especially his youth. That was only natural for her sex. On the other hand she admired Brecknock's address and qualifications, though he wore a long grey beard, possessed worn-out features, and had an ample reservoir of bigoted principles. In fact she wasn't at all sure but that in the end she would have to marry this Brecknock, for her father was greatly influenced by Fitzgerald, who no doubt would advance the interests of his friend.

The girl herself was exceedingly fascinating : of rather low stature, she was plump, well proportioned and voluptuous looking. Her jet black hair rivalled in depth of shade her sloe-coloured eyes. And those tempting lips of hers ! Her education was not very solid, still she could speak and write English passing well. She was tyrannised by a savage of a father. He drank copiously, cursed voluminously and thrashed his beautiful wife incessantly. He had won her from twenty rivals, and seemed to think that after such an achievement he was entitled to use her as he liked. Indeed on one occasion he acted unforgivingly towards her. It was after the Maidenhill Races, when, at a great ball given by him, he, through jealousy, struck her a blow that knocked her down on the floor ! She left him for some time, but her attachment to her daughter made her soon return. Then she was shut up within the confines of their residence for seven years, two guards having strict orders to see that she would not leave the grounds. Indeed both daughter and mother were cruelly treated by the drunken old glutton, who was incapable of showing any of the feelings of a father or husband.

D

So Hyacinth Martin was Timothy Brecknock's rival for the hand of Miss Anne O'Donel of Mossvale. Martin' to the great annoyance of Brecknock, used to pay frequent visits to Miss Anne O'Donel, and invariably passed through Turlough in making those visits. Brecknock fell on a plan to frighten the soul out of his rival, and thus deter him from continuing his attentions at Mossvale. The plan was this. George Robert and Brecknock decided that Andrew Craig, better known as Scotch Andy—dashing young blade whom Fitzgerald brought from the north of Ireland, and made his groom, and on whose sole testimony George Robert was afterwards convicted—and a fellow named Fulton should lie in ambush near the river-park and wait till Martin would be passing, when they should jump up, arrest him and bring him up before the magistrates, Fitzgerald and Brecknock, on the charge of attempting an assault. The instructions were given, and Fitzgerald put in the provision that no blood should be spilled.

One evening as the trap was laid, Martin was riding by this spot when Scotch Andy rushed out from his covert, snatched the horse's reins and tried to hold the horse ; Martin dealt Andy a blow between the eyes with the handle of a loaded whip, stunning him on the spot and knocking him down. Being thus free he galloped off, amid frequent shots from Fulton's blunderbuss. The plan proved a failure, and no one was more digusted with it than poor Brecknock. Martin rode to Castlebar and related the occurrence to Pat Randal McDonnel and others, and they were unanimous in condemning Fitzgerald for the affair. Martin's visits to Miss O'Donel were still frequent, and Brecknock determined to adopt bolder measures to put an end to them.

# Abduction of Miss O'Donel.

It was decided that her abduction should be effected. One night as Brecknock was giving full directions to Scotch Andy, Fulton and another, as to how it should be carried out, an old servant of Martin's named Davy Bourke overheard them ; he sets off to Grousehall, ten miles from Castlebar, and informs Martin. The latter, accompanied with Pat Randal and others, hastily repair to Mossvale, but the bird had flown. They were late ! They found the old father raging ; cursing like a devil, and deeply under the influence of strong liquors. He accused Martin and the whole gang with him ; they defended themselves and blamed Fitzgerald for it. "By the immaculate glory of Hell !" exclaimed the old debauchee, "he'll find O'Donel able to use a pistol as well as any fire-eater that ever boasted the name of Fitzgerald." They left him in this blaspheming mood, and proceeded to George Robert's house in Turlough. It was night-when they arrived there, and sleep reigned supreme in Turlough House. Martin knocked so loudly at the halldoor that he awakened Fitzgerald, who raised the window and demanded who dared to disturb his place that hour of the night. Martin charged him with having stolen away Miss O'Donel, and claimed her restoration. "A Martin again, if I live !" cried George Robert. Martin challenged him and asked him to come outside. George Robert threatened that if they weren't out of his demesne in ten minutes he'd discharge six pieces of ordnance from his fortress, and let loose wild bears on them.

These cannons he obtained from a Dutch vessel which was wrecked in the Newport Bay ; and the Government represented by the Lord Lieutenant, Earl Carlisle, despatched

Colonel Longfield soon after this affair with six companies of foot and two troops of cavalry and a train of artillery to dismantle the "fortress" George Robert was reported to have had ! Castlebar was then supplied for the first time with an artillery station.

Prudently enough the rescuers withdrew and permitted Fitzgerald to continue his repose undisturbed.   On the next day Ellison, a Justice of the Peace, proceeded to Fitzgerald's house, at the head of a company of dragoons, to inquire about the abduction.   George Robert laughed at the charge made, and expressed his surprise at Ellison paying any attention to what Davy Bourke swore in his "informations."   Nothing important occured till the day after, when a long array of magistrates sat and listened to Davy Bourke's story.   The confused and inconsistent version Bourke gave satisfied the bench that there was not a particle of truth in it.   On leaving the court Fitzgerald met old O'Donel, who had been presiding on the bench, and shook hands most cordially with him.   Martin challenged Fitzgerald in the court, and both were bound over to the peace.   Some while after this Pat Randal McDonnel arrested a man named Saultry for being party to the abduction.

## Attack on the Judges as they were leaving Castlebar after the Assizes.

Saultry was in prison till the Summer Assizes came round. The famous Tony Fimpster prosecuted and showed that he himself was the person Saultry employed to aid in the carrying out of the abduction, and that Saultry wrote the letter which trapped Miss Anne O'Donel.   The letter purported to be written by her lover, Martin, asking her to meet him on a certain night out in the demesne surrounding her home. She did come out at the appointed time, but instead of meeting her lover, encountered Brecknock's gang, who carried her off to Pontoon. Saultry was sentenced to imprisonment for life ! This severe sentence enraged his relatives who were tenants on Harry Lynch's estate near Balla. And to satisfy their desire for vengeance they determined to " have it out " with the judge who sentenced him.

As the two judges were leaving Castlebar where the assizes had been held, and had arrived at a small village called Minola or Manulla, about midway between Castlebar and Balla, to their astonishment further progress was blocked by a numerous crowd of peasants in menacing attitudes. Saultry's friends and many of the neighbours had assembled with sticks and stones in order to avenge Saultry's severe sentence. The judges commanded the escort to proceed and use violence if necessary, but the peasantry were too numerous to be scattered very easily. The escort was beaten and stoned ; the windows of the judges' carriages smashed ; the traces cut in pieces ; the horses' tails docked, and the judges terrified for their lives. The tenants then left the scene, and some hours elapsed before a fresh relay of horses could be obtained from Castlebar to enable the judges to proceed on their journey.

## Miss O'Donel concealed in Pontoon ; her Rescue.

Miss Anne O'Donel was conveyed straightway from her own residence in Mossvale to the shores of Lough Cullen, the smaller of the two lakes that beautify Pontoon. This locality is undoubtedly picturesque, and unanimously admired by tourists.    Fishing and shooting are to be got there.    As the tourist, travelling from Castlebar, has covered a lime-stone road of eight miles, and is nearing a curve on the road which the lake washes, all of a sudden a wild, romantic scene bursts on his view.    By the touch of a fairy's wand, as it were, a rude, magnificent picture strikes his vision.    Steep and rugged, thickly clad with heath and small brushwood, shoots up on the left the lofty hill of Cumner ; on the right extends Lough Cullen, ever gracious to the skilled angler ; in front, as if to veil the beauties yet in store, the rocky and cumberous hill, Benrievah, boldly takes its stand.    As you proceed towards Ballina, a bridge spans the meeting of the two lakes.    And to take a seat on the shore of Lough Conn with Benrievah at your back, you can feast yourself to excess on the wild grandeur of the scene.    You doubt that the watery expanse before you is a lake ; far as eye can run, water meets its view.    The shore, or rather coast, is rugged and angry looking ; huge rocks chiselled only by the hand of nature, are white with the foam of the charging billows when the storm rages.    The screams of wild birds in this lonely place are the first and almost the sole indication of animal life.    You see no intruding quadruped, for wood and rock form the only pasture ; you rarely meet a human being ; but to find a spot its equal in savage grandeur, rude magnificence, solitary splendour, or to observe nature so faithfully decked out in her own attire, you must visit Connemara, or perhaps the Highlands of Scotland, so vividly described by Sir Walter Scott.

Miss O'Donel passed the night in a cottage by the shore of Lough Cullen, and the next morning she was rowed from Cullen to Conn, and left in the custody of a Mr. Mitchell, who with his wife and daughter were the sole occupiers of an island in the middle of that vast lake. Miss O'Donel had not even the slightest notion as to the meaning of this abduction. The whole affair was to her a mystery, and though she fretted a good deal and felt depressed in spirits, the treatment she received at the hands of the Mitchell family was kind, generous and attentive.

One night when no one but Mrs. Mitchell and Anne O'Donel were in the house, Brecknock landed on the island, fully resolved to force marriage. He was soaked with whiskey and wine, and thereby deprived of his usual discretion and sense of honour. He entered Miss O'Donel's room with a lighted candle in his hand, and staggered towards the bed where she was sleeping ; the noise awoke her, and she half dreaming and half sensible, rushed for her cloak, screaming for help. He caught hold of her and begged her to consent to be Mrs. Brecknock, and finally threatened he would there on the spot rob her of her virtue if she didn't consent. Being so very much under the influence of drink, she easily escaped his grasp. She seized a rusty musket from over the door and swore she'd shoot him if he'd advance one step. Brecknock retreated slowly towards the door, blew the candle out, and rushed at the unprotected maiden. He pulled the gun from her and would have deprived her of what Irish maidens prize more highly than life, when voices and footsteps were heard in the house.

Brecknock hadn't time to carry out his evil purpose, but hurried out a back-door and had barely reached the boat awaiting him on the shore when Martin was searching the house to blow the brains out of the shameless old villain. Martin, through his ceaseless efforts, had discovered at last where his beloved now was hid, and arrived in time to stave off dishonour.   He found her in a swoon.   After some time she recovered, or as the country folks say "came to," and Martin conducted her back to her parents.   Soon after her father was on his death-bed ; and happily for him, he was enabled, through the aid of Father Lennon, to die penitent ; before breathing his last, however, he consented to give Anne as wife to Martin, and the marriage came of six months later.

## The Murder of Pat Randal McDonnel.

A few weeks previous to the restoration of Miss O'Donel to her parents, a strange incident occurred which formed the commencement of a very tragic affair.   It led up to the foul murder of Pat Randal McDonnel, Colonel of the Mayo Volunteer corps, and to the execution of George Robert Fitzgerald, in Castlebar Jail.

One evening Pat Randal was proceeding home to Chancery Hall, when a shot was fired some hundred yards from Turlough demesne, and the bullet hit him in the leg, just below the knee.   He accused a man named Murphy, one of George Robert's servants ; and George Robert in turn accused Pat Randal of assaulting Murphy, and swore information to that effect before Mr. O'Malley, Justice of the Peace.   Fitzgerald brought with him his Turlough corps to Castlebar, and paraded up and down the main street, on the look out for Pat Randal, in order to arrest him.   The latter soon appeared at the head of the Mayo legion, and encountered the Turlough force on the bridge at the end of the main street.   A short struggle took place, which ended in driving the followers of Fitzgerald off the scene, and compelling himself to run into one of the shops for protection. He thus failed to capture Pat Randal on that occasion; but a few days later, February 19th, 1786, told a sadder tale. Fitzgerald heard that Pat Randal was at home this evening, entertaining his friends Hipson and Andrew Gallagher. Coming on morning he, with Fulton and his followers, surrounded the house in Chancery Hall, broke in the front door, and inquired for McDonnel. The answer given by the terrified servant was that her master was not at home. Fulton entered with two warrants, and arrested Hipson and Gallagher; and after a long, careful search, discovered Pat Randal, who was concealed in some barley that was lying at the back of the house.

Fitzgerald's followers were only too anxious to get an opportunity of wreaking their vengeance on the three, for they had not yet forgotten the thrashing they had received a few days previous in Castlebar at the hands of the Volunteers. Fitzgerald, however, prevented any violence being used, and ordered the three, Hipson, Gallagher, and McDonnel to be conveyed to Turlough Castle. There they were quartered for the night in a top room, and guarded by four armed henchmen of George Robert's. The latter sent word to Pat Randal inquiring if he would have some refreshments, but McDonnel refused firmly. George Robert came up himself and pressed Pat Randal, saying: " Damn it, McDonnel, though you always treated me vilely, and though the same county can't contain you and me, yet the hospitality of Turlough House shall not be disgraced." He left, and got a servant to bring up to Pat Randal a bottle of champagne, some cold wild-fowl, and a snug, warm bed, luxuries denied to the other two.

Miss O'Donel had not as yet left the lone island in

Lough Conn, where she had been conveyed at the command of Brecknock ; so no one had the least knowledge as to her whereabouts, or as to the cause of her disappearance. The ingenious charge preferred against McDonnel and the other two was that they " illegally imprisoned Miss Anne O'Donel, and burglariously entered her domicile." This was the composition of the lawyer, Timothy Brecknock, and he informed Fitzgerald that this offence amounted to a felony, and that it was lawful to shoot down anyone attempting to rescue persons accused of felony. Now it does not appear that Fitzgerald at all desired the death of McDonnel, or was a party to the plot that resulted in the cruel massacre we are about to relate.

Fitzgerald, however, gave orders that the three prisoners should be brought to Castlebar, and there charged with the felony already mentioned. Twenty well-armed servants of George Robert's were to convey the three accused to Castlebar, and they had strict injunctions to shoot the prisoners if there was any attempt at rescue. Pat Randal McDonnel, Hipson, and Andrew Gallagher, surrounded by guards, proceeded, under the leadership of Scotch Andy, otherwise Craig, towards Castlebar. McDonnel being unable to walk from the painful wound in his leg already referred to, was supplied with a horse which a servant named Murphy, with drawn sword, led by the bridle ; Hipson and Gallagher were tied together with a rope, arm to arm. The procession had advanced just a quarter of a mile from Turlough on its way to Castlebar, when a shot was fired from inside the wall. "A Rescue, a rescue," shouted Scotch Andy. " Down with the prisoners ! Bullet them at once !" Thereupon a savage butchery ensued. The three unprotected prisoners were at the mercy of twenty ruffians

who, every man of them, were armed with loaded guns.
Triggers were pulled, and charges fired.    Hipson's body was
perforated with slugs, and the rope that bound him and
Gallagher together was torn with bullets.    Gallagher's wrist
was pierced through, and his knee severely wounded ; he
rolled forward and tumbled, unperceived, into a ditch half full
of water and bushes.    McDonnel's right arm was broken,
and what saved him at the time was that the murderers
couldn't get a fair shot at him, as Murphy, who was well
occupied in struggling with the plunging horse, was in risk
of being hit.

Despite Murphy's efforts to control the terrified animal, it
burst from his hands and dashed away at a furious pace
with Pat Randal tied to the saddle, and didn't stop its head-
long flight till it arrived at a place called Gurtnafullah, Field
of Blood, near Kilnecarra Bridge, quite close to McDonnel's
own residence, Chancery Hall.    Here a country gossoon
rushed out before the runaway horse and stopped it.
McDonnel, quite exhausted, fell on the road.    He uttered a
few words, begging a little water for the love of God ; and
while the youngster was procuring it up came Craig (Scotch
Andy) panting and blowing.    The fiend coolly levels his
blunderbuss at poor McDonnel; the latter, helpless and half
stupid from the intense agony he was so manfully bearing,
cried out for merc : "Andrew, Andrew, only spare my life,
and you'll never want while I breathe."

"If you were my mother, by heavens, you'll have the
contents of this," replied Craig, and he discharged two
barrels, one breaking Pat Randal's other arm, and the
second shot tearing through his neck !    The corpse of
the gallant Colonel of the Mayo Volunteers, their favourite
and leader, lay unrecognised on the public road till the

next day, when Martin, who received information about
the butchery, arrived. As he bent down to kiss the
cold forehead of his truest friend, hot tears rolled
freely down his cheeks and his heart was ready to crack
with grief. " McDonnel," exclaimed Martin, " is this your
end ! What a noble soul you were, and is this the
death you deserved ! " Martin had the body conveyed
to Chancery Hall, and then rode to Castlebar to inform the
Volunteers. On the return of Scotch Andy from his foul
deed he espied Gallagher lying in the ditch ; he came down
off his horse, put Gallagher in the saddle, and brought him
directly to Turlough Castle. When he arrived there,
Fitzgerald, who appeared very excited, deplored the whole
affair and endeavoured to provide every comfort for
Gallagher ; his wounds were dressed, food and drink ordered,
and a few hours spent in a very confidential chat. The
result was that Gallagher promised not to give evidence at
all in the matter. Whether the firing of the shot from behind
the wall was pre-arranged by Fitzgerald and Brecknock it does
not appear ; but there is little doubt at all events that Scotch
Andy knew something about it. The Mayo Volunteers were
now in view, and it was evident that a great number of
McDonnel's friends were accompanying the legion over which
he had been Colonel. Fitzgerald was urged and persuaded
to take a horse and escape ; he attempted three times to
mount, but failed in each effort ! He was absolutely unnerved
and paralysed. The soldiers arrived at the house, entered
it and captured Brecknock and Fulton. After prolonged
search they found Fitzgerald buried in a chest of clothes ;
and only for the presence of Mr. Ellison, Justice of the
Peace, George Robert would have been torn limb from limb
by the infuriated followers of Pat Randal McDonnel. The

fine house was pillaged; furniture, ornaments, and immense quantities of linen which was stored away in some of the spare rooms, all fell into the hands of the fortunate plunderers. Craig (Scotch Andy) escaped for the present, but was afterwards arrested near Dublin. The three prisoners were conducted to Castlebar Jail where they were accommodated with separate cells.

## George Robert's vile treatment in Castlebar Prison.

George Robert was confined in a single room all to himself; and two armed soldiers kept guard. In the middle of the night, the Sub-Sheriff, an enemy of Fitzgerald's, withdrew one of the sentries to another portion of the jail, and thereupon a preconcerted attack was made on Fitzgerald in his cell. The sole guard, McBeth, was knocked down, and deprived of his gun; a crowd of angry looking men rushed upon the solitary and defenceless captive. They had pistols, sword canes, solid stumps of blackthorns, and all were liberally applied to Fitzgerald. Some of the shots lodged in his thigh; the little finger of his left hand was broken; he was battered with sticks, and dragged around the prison like a dead dog. A thrust of a bayonet pierced his arm, and two of his front teeth were smashed as he stopped a sword cane from piercing his throat! He defended himself with all the strength and daring of a man fighting for his life. His strength soon began to leave him, and this was an invitation for a more vehement onslaught; pistol-butts and thumps were again savagely applied, till at last—" Cowardly rascals, you may now leave off; you have finished me; I'm no match for you," cried Fitzgerald, and

he lay down senseless.   The assassins left, satisfied that the
" fire-eater " was extinct.   However, the authorities come at
them, but all got off scot free !   It would be useless to
speculate on the motives that gave rise to this dastardly
attack on Fitzgerald.   It might have been caused by
personal spite, or it might have been a sort of vengeance
wreaked on him for the murder of McDonnel, and done
through a suspicion that he would not be convicted;
whatever was the cause, there is no other way of
characterising the deed than that of pronouncing it a
cowardly, ruffianly, and murderous act.

# CHAPTER IV.

Character—Trial—Speech of Fitzgerald in the Dock—Asserts his
Innocence—Sentence—Execution of Brecknock and Fulton—
Terrible Scene at the Execution of George Robert—The Appeal
of George Robert.

# Trial and Execution of George Robert Fitzgerald.

WE are now entering upon the fourth and last chapter of
our story. In it the hero of the preceding pages will be
brought to the bar of justice, twelve jurymen will brand
him with their verdict as a murderer ; he will expiate his
crime-on the scaffold, and though many will sympathise
with him in his misfortune few will feel that he received
more than his deserts. Trying him according to the
standard of morality existing in his times, his most ardent
admirers and industrious apologists will be forced to admit
that he was a non-conformer. The lawless acts, the insulting affronts, and high-handed conduct of Fitzgerald won
from his partisans expressions of unwonted admiration,
eulogy, and applause, but brought on himself a reward in
this world which was just. Society was in danger while
such a man lived. We are not too severe, we believe, in
forming this opinion of the character of George Robert
Fitzgerald. His youth, his accomplishments, his high
connections, and his manly, honourable spirit plead very
strongly at the historian's tribunal, and almost extort a

mitigated sentence ; but, on the other hand, we cannot dispel
from our minds the evil influence he exercised in Mayo
throughout his short life ; the principal part he filled in
throwing that county into a state of chaotic confusion and
in keeping the sea angry when the tempest had subsided ;
finally, the part he played in the murder of McDonnel.
These latter considerations compel us to arrive at the con-
clusion already stated—that George Robert Fitzgerald, of
Turlough, deserved death at the hands of the common
hangman.

We saw him last in the prison cell ; now we shall proceed
with the sad history.

February 19th was the day on which the murder of Pat
Randal McDonnel was committed, and the March Assizes
following saw the prisoner arraigned.   Fitzgerald was so
severely wounded by the assault made on him in jail that he
had to be conveyed on a pallet from the prison to the courthouse.   His appearance was so sickly and his health so
weak that on Dr. Boyd's recommendation the trial was
postponed for a few months, till June 10th, 1786, when
Chief Baron Yelverton and Baron Power opened the Commission.   The Attorney-General, Fitzgibbon, a bitter enemy
of Fitzgerald's, conducted the prosecution.   The jury con-
sisted of—Thomas Lindsay, of Hollymount ; Smith Steel,
of Foxford ; James Lynch, of Cullen ; John Moore, of
Ballintaffy ; James Gildea, of Crosslough ; John Joyce, of
Oxford ; William Ousley, of Rushbrook ; Thomas Ormsby,
of Ballinamore ; Joseph Lambert, of Togher ; William
Ellison, of Tallyho ; Christopher Baynes, of Lakeland ;
and James Miller, of Westport.   George Robert was
arraigned for " having with another wilfully, traitorously,
and feloniously provoked, stirred up and procured Andrew

Craig and a number of others to slay and murder Pat Randal M'Donnel and Charles Hipson." Edward Stanley was counsel for Fitzgerald, and argued forcibly for the prisoner. He pointed out the unfairness and novelty of receiving the evidence of the actual murderer (Andrew Craig) against an accessory ; and also the anomaly of perhaps convicting the accessory while the principals might be acquitted. The principals were not tried till the following Monday, Fitzgerald being on his trial throughout the whole of Saturday. The Chief Baron was so much impressed with Stanley's objections that he proposed to Fitzgibbon to discharge the jury and try the principals first. To this Fitzgibbon refused to comply and succeeded in having the objections overruled. Throughout the case the Attorney-General frequently exhibited his enmity for the prisoner, and appeared jubilant in having his foe a degraded criminal in the dock ! He called names to Mr. Stanley, and once alluded to him as Mr. Tautology Puzzle-cause.

The witnesses came forward and the following evidence was substantially given :—

Andrew Gallagher proved the circumstances of the attack near Turlough, and how Craig brought him on horseback to Turlough House. Scotch Andy, or Craig, corroborated the evidence of Gallagher, and in addition swore that Fitzgerald gave directions to "shoot the covey ! Dead dogs tell no tales." He admitted quite coolly that he himself shot McDonnel. Those statements were supported by another of the accomplices, and by his own voluntary confession to a magistrate near Dublin. The defence was something like this. There were three warrants issued for the arrest of McDonnel, and in the possession of Fulton. Mr. Love swore he saw twelve armed followers of Pat Randal's inside

E

the wall near where the murder occurred, waiting for the prisoner to pass; and that he heard them say that if McDonnel was amongst those arrested, they would soon free him by shooting Fitzgerald and his bloody northerners; that soon after they fired from behind the wall, and thereupon a cry of murder was heard; that he stole off unperceived.

The Chief Baron charged the jury, remarking that though Love's evidence was very startling, yet Fitzgerald's men acted illegally in firing at the prisoners, since they offered no resistance to arrest, or attempted no escape. He recommended the jury to give the prisoner the benefit of any weighty doubt that might be pressing on their minds.

The jury retired, and were eagerly watched by Fitzgerald, who retained utter composure throughout the trial. In less than a quarter of an hour they returned and handed in a verdict of guilty ! A dead silence seized the court, an electric flash of pallor shot across George Robert's features, and a violent twitching of his mouth was apparent to all observers. The judge deferred passing sentence till Monday, and Fitzgerald spent the Sabbath in his cell.

On Monday, the 12th June, the principals in the murder were tried, and five, including Fulton, were convicted and hanged. Brecknock was put on his trial now and assumed the innocent lamb all through the ordeal. In his very soul he was a hypocrite, and a deeply-dyed one. He begged leave to say a few prayers before the prosecution should commence; after a few moments he rose from his knees and addressed the court. He claimed first a *medietas linguæ* jury, that is a jury composed of men speaking the same language as the accused. Brecknock being English, objected to an Irish jury. Chief Baron said, " This is wasting

time. The people of England and Ireland have one common language, and are governed by one common sovereign ;
and let it not go abroad that Englishmen are considered as
aliens in Ireland. Englishmen inherit in Ireland, and *vice
versa.* Both countries have the same laws, the same constitution, the same happy Government." Brecknock asked
to see if the bill of indictment was signed by the jury, but
was refused ; then he asserted that Gallagher was an incom-
petent witness, as he fled from justice :   " Desert your idle
babble and leave yourself in   the   hands of your able
counsel," said Baron Power.   The evidence, similar to
what convicted Fitzgerald, secured a like verdict in the case
of Brecknock.

Edward Stanley now proposed to move in arrest of judgment for George Robert Fitzgerald, and if this succeeded
the prisoner would be discharged. However, Baron Power
observed that really the only serious objection on the part
of the defence was now got rid of, by the conviction of the
principals, so there was no use proceeding with the motion.
Brecknock was asked what he had to say why the sentence
of death should not be passed on him, and he repeated the
same objections already cited. Baron Yelverton solemnly
and impressively delivered the following judgment on
Timothy Brecknock :   " Prisoner at the bar, if it is possible
there can be any degree of guilt beyond the crime of which
Mr. Fitzgerald is convicted, it remaineth with you, Timothy
Brecknock ; for under the colour of the law you devised a
wicked and artful scheme to commit a horrid and barbarous
murder. The laws of the land demand your life as a just
forfeit for the blood which has been shed ; and those
deluded wretches whom you inveigled into your plot, and
whom you deceived under hopes of safety, to become

the instruments of your horrid designs, are objects of pity when compared with the magnitude of your guilt. You made their ignorance the means of your purposes. Unfortunate old man ! happy had it been for you that you never had known law at all, or that you had known it better. Miserable man ! you are now the victim of your own subtleties and become the dupe of your own cunning. The venerable appearance you have assumed, and the sanctity you affect are, I fear, put on as a disguise for the conceal- ment of your wickedness. The law which you endeavoured to pervert, has furnished the detection of your crime, and will shortly award the punishment which attends your conviction. Your jury, from a mistaken lenity, have recom- mended you to mercy, through pity for your age and infirmities. Your crime is, by many degrees, of the deepest and blackest die, and it only remains for me to pronounce the dreadful sentence." The awful sentence of death was then pronounced and the execution was announced to take place that very day. No visible change appeared on Brecknock's countenance throughout this scene ; he was perfectly absorbed in devout prayer from beginning to end, and seemed unconscious or indifferent to the surroundings.

The Chief Baron, after passing sentence on Brecknock, addressed Fitzgerald in those words : " Prisoner in the dock, you have been found guilty of the murder of Patrick Randal McDonnel by twelve men sworn on their oaths, and the sentence awarded by law for that crime is death. Even Providence has interposed that justice might not be disap- pointed, and in the midst of murder preserved the life of one man as a witness for the discovery of your crime. The hand of God protected your life from assassination, that it might be offered up as a sacrifice on the altar of public justice. Your tender daughter, the offspring of your loins ; your wife, the inconsolable partner of your bed, partake of your disgrace. You came into the world with the advantages of talents, which, if properly cultivated, would have carried you through life with respectability and honour. Blest with the recommendation of birth and fortune ; allied to great and respectable connections ; possessed of every qualification requisite to render you an ornament to society, and a valuable member of the community, you are now sunk to the lowest extremity of human infamy and shame. It is my duty to pronounce to you the dreadful sentence of the law "——.

Here Fitzgerald interrupted and said : " I beg leave to trouble your lordships with a few words. I do not mean to cast blame anywhere. I accuse no one. From the evidence, the jury could have found no other verdict ; and of course you, my lords, must deliver the sentence prescribed by law. I did not think such evidence would be produced ; if I had known it, I could have been better prepared. There are some family affairs which are half settled, and I would ask your lordships to give me the opportunity of having them completed before I leave this world. However guilty I may be conceived within a narrow circle, I hope in a higher one, the unprejudiced part of the world will think me innocent ; those who know me from my earliest life, know me incapable of such an action.

" I never feared death ; nor am I afraid to meet it in any shape ; in the most formidable, even an ignominious death. It may be thought I wish to solicit pardon,—I would not accept pardon after being found guilty by such a jury, because I know I could not face the world after it. It has been suggested, and I understand the report prevails, I wish for time in order to commit suicide.  As a worldly man I never feared death ; and as a Christian, which I hope I am, and a good one, what sort of a passport would that be to the place of eternity ?  I forgive every one,

## and though I assert my innocence,

I do not mean to say I have no sins : I have many, which overwhelm me, and I only request time, that I may make my peace with God."

The Chief Baron resumed his judgment.  "It is not in our power to grant your request.  We are not the dispensers of mercy.  Your offence is of such a nature that my brother judge and myself thought ourselves justified to have ordered immediate execution ; nevertheless, from the hope that you might be better prepared to meet your fate with becoming penitence you have been allowed two days. If by time now, you mean a few hours, I am sure the Sheriff will show you every humanity.  It is my duty, and I call on God and heaven to witness, that it is the most painful one I ever performed, to pronounce the dreadful sentence of the law."

They were to be hanged before sunset on that day. Brecknock and Fulton were conveyed in a cart from the old Jail then at the corner of Castle Lane meeting Ellison Street, to the new Jail on the "Green" then in process of completion.  The fine brick building of the Bank of Ireland now occupies that spot.  It was generally rumoured in Castlebar that after this bank was finished, noises like the slapping of doors and closing of windows were heard night after night for several months ; and that such noises were attributed to the fact of the place having been the witness to so many executions.  Brecknock dressed in careful manner, his beard and locks neatly arranged, appeared to be an innocent martyr, though there was not one heart amidst the vast crowds moved to pity for the criminal.  Fulton seemed already a corpse; his pale face, shivering limbs, and craving-for-mercy looking expression excited much merriment.  On the scaffold he made a clear full confession to his clergyman.  He acknowledged that his sentence was just ; stated that Fitzgerald did not give orders for the murder, but that Scotch Andy was the sole cause of the dreadful massacre.  Both now were absorbed in prayer; and in a few moments white caps were put down over their heads, the ropes around their necks adjusted, and in the next moment Brecknock and Fulton were swinging lifeless in the air amidst the cheers of a not very sympathetic gathering.

We have described the character of Hyacinth Martin who married Miss Anne O'Donel a short time after her father's death.  Craig died a year after this scene, wasting away in prison of a loathsome itch.  Fulton and Brecknock were sent to the next world ; and it only remains for us, in order to round off the history of George Robert Fitzgerald, to relate, though reluctantly, the sad scene of his execution.

## Execution of George Robert.

About six o'clock in the evening of Monday, June 12th, 1786, George Robert Fitzgerald was led from his cell to the scaffold.  The other prisoners had been executed by this time.  He left the old Jail then situate at corner of Castle

Lane and Ellison Street and walked up Castle Lane to the new Jail then in process of completion, but now replaced by the Bank of Ireland. Fitzgerald hurriedly walked through Castle Lane surrounded by crowds of young and old, all sympathising with him. His person was carelessly and negligently attired, his garments soiled and torn; his face pale and haggard, with fierce red eyes flashing wildly around; his hair tossed and matted. In this frantic condition of mind and body he hastened to the fatal spot and asked in shaking accents, " Is this the place ? "

As he stood on the scaffold, his arms and feet were secured; the white cap was put on, and the rope adjusted on his neck. There the great fire-eater stood facing a scene of unparalleled excitement and of historic interest.

An excited sea of upturned faces moved in front. All eyes were rivetted on the culprit. The street in front of the scaffold was lined with military, the 66th regiment being then stationed in Castlebar, and a large reinforcement was sent to the town for the occasion, as it was feared a rescue would be attempted. Denis Browne astride his horse and in the company of his sub-sheriff, rode up and down between the two lines of armed red-coats. Bayonets were drawn. The excitement was intense. The hour had come and Fitzgerald was plunged into eternity ! Not so soon, however ; for the sudden jerk of his body snapped the cord, and down he fell some thirty feet. A deep murmur rose from the vast assembly, and voices, not a few, were heard to utter the words, " Let him off," " Give him his liberty." As he was brought up a second time, "Cannot the Sheriff supply me with a rope strong enough ? " said Fitzgerald, reappearing on the scaffold. " You'll have one soon," replied Denis Erowne, "and be sure, Clarke (the Sub-sherriff), to get a strong one." The interval was passed in prayers; his clergyman, Rev. Mr. Henry, giving him all the comforts and aid religion alone can give when the last moments of life are rapidly ebbing away. A new rope was brought, and, strange to say, the professional hangman refused to perform his duty ; in his place a convict, who had been released for his services, secured Fitzgerald with the fresh rope and drew the bolt. Instantly George Robert dropped, and instead of swinging in the air, fell to the ground again. The job was botched. He was severely hurt; his leg coming under him in the fall was broken. " My life is my own," exclaimed the suffering, and I may say dying man. "Not while there's a rope in Castlebar, Ballina, or Westport," roared the Sheriff, Denis Browne, foaming with rage. Now the excitement was beyond measure. The evening had already come on, and darkness was rapidly creeping over the scenè. As the tortured prisoner was carried to the scaffold the third time the mass of horrified human beings began to disperse ; a whisper grew into a report, a report assumed the size of common belief, and all saw or thought they saw threatening figures in the air ; thunder crashed, and peal after peal rolled in the sky ; purple lightning flared and flashed ; hailstones came down with fury and force; the crowd, paralysed with dread, scattered in a few moments. Fitzgerald was thrown off the third time ; he struggled a little but soon hung a corpse, presenting a ghastly lead-colour appearance in the blue gleam the sudden and frequent streaks of lightning threw on the scene.

It is a popular belief that the High Sheriff, Right Hon. Denis Browne, had in his possession, the day of the execution, the reprieve of George Robert. A message had been sent to the Castle, on Saturday, the day of his conviction, for the purpose of obtaining pardon ; and it would not be unlikely that Fitzgerald's high connection would have been a strong point in his favour.

Fitzgerald's body was conveyed to Turlough and interred in the family vault, which is within the old Abbey close by the Round Tower. His bones were raised on the occasion of his brother's interment, and a ring was discovered on George Robert's finger ; this was for a long time in the possession of a man named Ritchie. His heart-broken wife entered a convent, and his only child, a daughter by the first wife, died early of grief.

We have now reached the end of our history, and related the career of George Robert Fitzgerald ; beginning with his birth, watching his life in Connaught and on the Continent, closing with his execution and burial. The famous appeal is a document of such an interesting nature that we make bold to introduce to our readers some few extracts from it. It is a document of antiquarian interest ; and it is somewhat difficult to obtain a copy of it. In the King's Inns Library, Dublin, and in the Royal Irish Academy, I have seen the entire Appeal. It is the production of a gentleman of literary tastes, but shows no proofs of extensive knowledge or of high literary culture.

A leading King's counsel talking to Baron Yelverton on his return to Dublin after the trial, said, "Well, Baron, though Fitzgerald got no more than he deserved, yet the murderer was murdered!"

## Excerpts from George Robert Fitzger- ald's famous appeal which he wrote while in prison.

"Nor did I take simple possession of the estate and after- wards instantly fly away from my demense to spend the rents of it in Dublin, London, Paris, or in Rome.  On the contrary my stationary residence—a residence, not there to sot and doze away in unmeaning dulness and inactive stupidity, a life burdensome to myself and useless to my fellow-creatures. I had informed myself from different vouchers that we rarely, if ever, have a greater quantity of bread-corn in this island than will hold out for more than six or seven weeks' con- sumption : the inference I drew was that, if the naval power of the House of Bourbons should continue to be superior to that of Great Britain, we should then lie at the mercy of France for our bread-corn, and two million five hundred thousand souls might, any time in three or four months, be reduced to the unavoidable necessity of surrendering at dis- cretion to the armies of Louis XVI. without firing a single cannon, notwithstanding the powerful armies now on foot for the defence of this kingdom.   For I had determined in my own breast to bring these two articles of bread-corn and wheaten-flour to great perfection, and in as great a plenty as they are in our sister kingdom England.   While I was thus setting an humble though, perhaps, laudable example of agriculture and useful husbandry to my compatriot nobility and gentry at large, I did not omit giving every possible attention and encouragement to the principal commodity of this country, I mean the manufacture of Irish linen in all its various branches. This important article of internal con-sumption and foreign export having fallen by the calamity of the present war under its intrinsic real value, I purchased all the linens made by my own tenantry and for four miles round about my neighbourhood, giving a halfpenny a yard above the market price, and thus preserved this important, this national article of commerce from languishing and pass-ing away, which otherwise must soon have been the case had the manufacturers experienced the utter impossibility of acquiring a subsistence by it.

" Not a day labourer in my own extensive manor, not a carpenter, mason, or architectonic artist for miles round me but, winter and summer, were constantly employed. Never less than fifty, and generally a hundred and fifty persons of one denomination or other daily partook of my bounty and punctually received the wages of industry. In one year on my ground were planted no less than ten thousand timber trees, and thirty thousand acorns —a future navy! *crescens in occulto* Two hundred acres of land for wheat had been already brought under the dominion of the plough ; and had I not been deprived of my liberty, I had laid out for this and every succeeding year four hundred acres for the sole culture and growth of bread-corn ; an example which, if copied to an equal extent by only five hundred gentlemen, could not fail to secure us from the insidious, keen ever intriguing views and naval force of France. Nor stopped I here, but having remarked the grittiness, coarseness and muddy colour of our best wheaten flour, which I attributed to the bad apparatus of our mills, I appropriated twenty-five hundred pounds to the erection of a mill, now wholly finished, all but its covering in, and fitted it up with the choicest stones for grinding, brought at great expense from France, none being equal to them in any part of Europe. If I did thus widely spread my wings abroad, let it be remembered I did not desert nor forget my own little nest at home; for plenty without profusion adorned my tables, good order and sobriety reigned among my numerous servants, the gates of hospitality were opened alike to rich and poor, while morning and evening prayers, daily administered under my roof, seemed to have drawn down from heaven the invaluable blessings of harmony, content, and peace."

Referring to Judge Carleton, who imprisoned him and fined him for illtreating his father, Fitzgerald writes : " He was only a judge *fait à hâte*, and consequently, like most other upstarts, especially when they are men of very scanty abilities, might find himself in an awkward position, and be all the while under one continued confusion of ideas and perturbation of mind. The public will perceive my great tenderness for his character ; they will perceive that I could not descend so low as to bear any animosity against him, and that I have not absolutely charged him with having given a corrupt judgment. God and he both know whether the judgment be corrupt or only an erroneous one. I do not positively and in direct terms charge him on the score of a corrupt judgment. *Le jeu ne vaut pas la chandelle.* I know very well that such a charge must, upon conviction of the young man, affect him in body, lands and goods. But in what respect should I be the gainer by his conviction ? As to his goods, I assure him they are not an object to me. I am too much the Christian to desire or covet them. As to his lands, I believe neither he nor any of his progenitors were ever seized

of a forty-shilling freehold.   And with regard to his body, I
can reasonably have no wish to defraud or delay the corporation of crows, or that of worms, of a luscious repast,
which though probably they consider as their just due, yet
I do not ambition the office of being their caterer, much
less that of their carver.   I own the picture which Virgil
hath drawn of a certain judge, who first punished and then
heard the persons who had the misfortune to be brought
before his bar, pressed strongly on my mind, and I could
not but think there was a striking likeness between Mr.
Carleton and Rhadamanthus.

'Gnossius haec Rhadamanthus habet,
                    durissima jura,
    Castigata audita dolos.'

"Mr. Carleton, you are now no longer a Judge of Oyer
and Terminer.   Your short-lived phætonic career is at an
end.   The character of Judge sat ill upon you.   We know
it was an assumed and not your natural one.   But that
farce is now over—the curtain is fallen, and you and I are
once more upon a level, mere private individuals."

"It is notoriously known from one end of the county
Mayo to the other that there is much ill blood of long standing between the Fitzgeralds and Brownes of that county.   I
leave it, therefore, to the public to judge whether Lord
Altamount's house was a proper place for Mr. Sergeant
Browne and Mr. Carleton to dine, knowing in their con-
sciences they were both to sit in judgment upon me the
very next day.   Let us then suppose this new-fashioned
nobleman should have no objection after supper to a little
party at cards.   What an entertaining *parti quarré* must it
have been, all four laying their wise heads together, and,

perhaps, my identical self the sole topic of their conversation."

The inscription of the Fitzgeralds' family tomb in Turlough is this :—

" Here lieth the body of Thomas Fitzgerald, Esqre. He ended a life of as few failings and as many virtues as ever fell to the share of man, the 15th day of July, 1747, in the 86th year of his age. He was son and heir of John Fitzgerald, of Gorteen, in the County Waterford, where his ancestors and he enjoyed great possessions, as well as in the County of Kilkenny, from the landing of Strongbow, in the reign of Henry II., A.D. 1111, to the time of his transplantation to Mayo. He first married Elizabeth Ferron, mother of Ralp Jemison, Esq., Master of the Buckhounds to his Majesty George II. He afterwards married Henrietta Browne, daughter to John Browne, of the Neal, Esq., by whom he had Elizabeth, John, George, Nicholas, Julia, Henry, Mary Cecilia, Bridget, Edward, and Michael, of which only married, George to the Right Honourable Lady Mary Hevry, sister to the Right Honourable the Earl of Bristol ; Mary to the Marquess d'Arezzo, Governor of Naples, and Nicholas to Margaret Stephenson, daughter to James Stephenson, of Killylagh, Esqre , and Bridget to Thomas Lyster, Esqre., of Grange.''

FINIS.